THE OFFICIAL
DUNE
COLOURING BOOK

INSPIRED BY
FRANK HERBERT'S *DUNE*

GOLLANCZ

LONDON

ILLUSTRATED BY

TOMISLAV TOMIĆ

COLOURED BY

I must not fear.
Fear is the mind-killer.
Fear is the little-death that
brings total obliteration.
I will face my fear.
I will permit it to pass
over me and through me.
And when it has gone past,
I will turn the inner eye
to see its path.
Where the fear has gone
there will be nothing.
Only I will remain.

REVEREND MOTHER
GAIUS HELEN MOHIAM

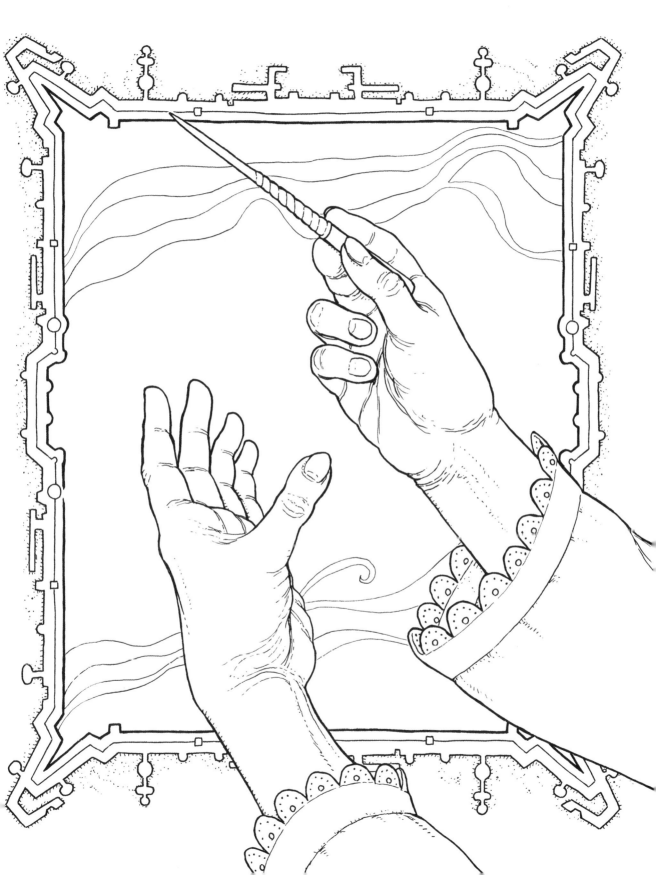

DUKE LETO ATREIDES

EMPEROR SHADDAM IV

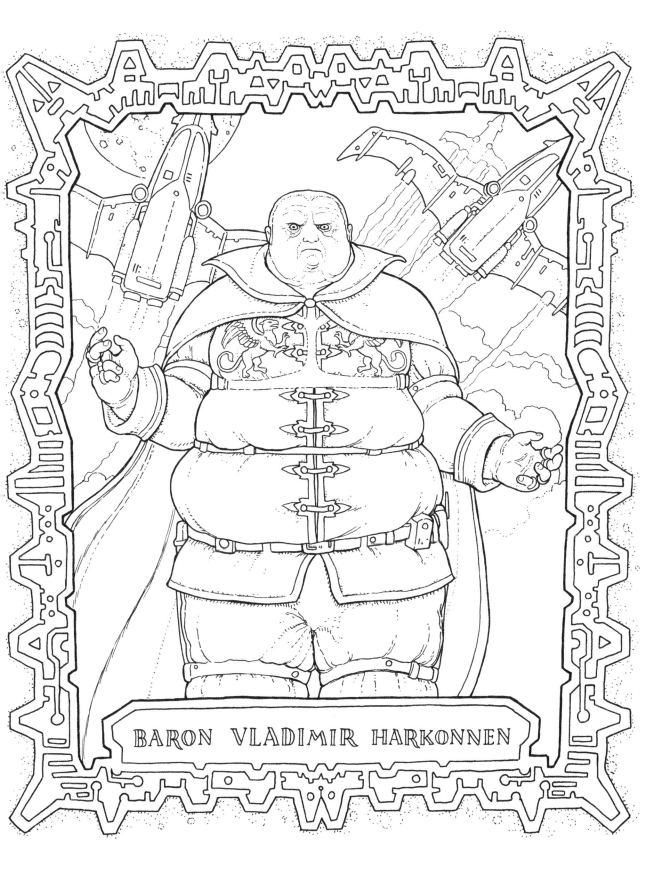

BARON VLADIMIR HARKONNEN

GURNEY HALLECK

LADY JESSICA

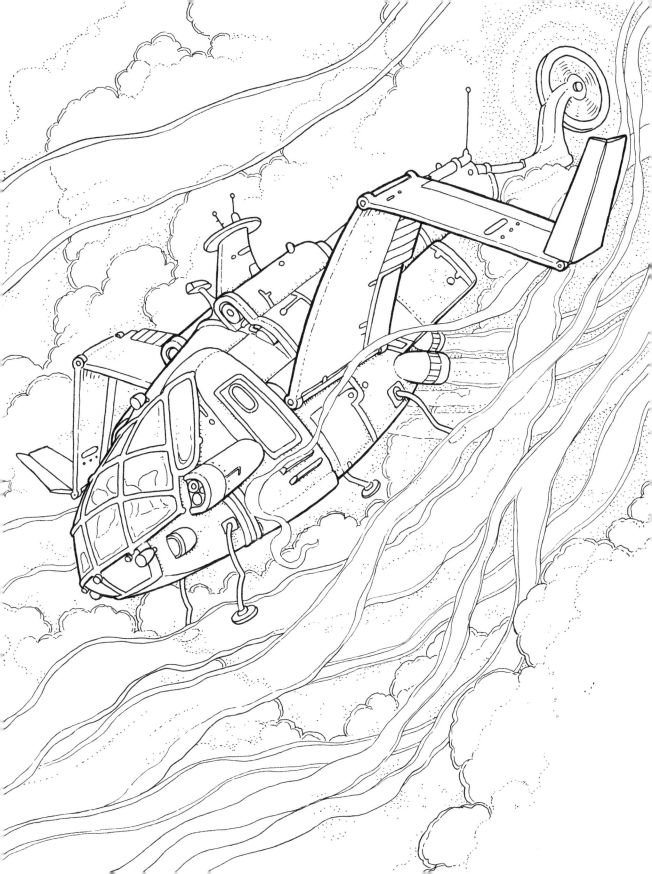

CHANI

STILGAR

FEYD-RAUTHA HARKONNEN

ALIA ATREIDES

PRINCESS IRULAN

PAUL ATREIDES

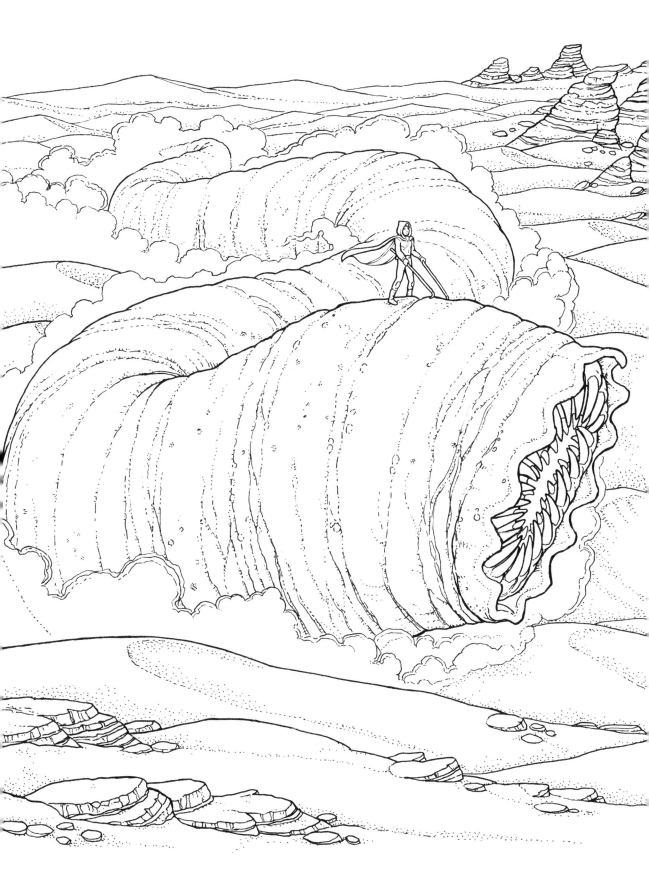

First published in Great Britain in 2023 by Gollancz
an imprint of The Orion Publishing Group Ltd
Carmelite House, 50 Victoria Embankment
London EC4Y 0DZ

An Hachette UK Company

10 9 8 7 6 5 4 3 2 1

A CIP catalogue record for this book is
available from the British Library.

ISBN (Paperback) 978 1 399 62009 3

Printed in Italy

www.gollancz.co.uk